Not AR 10-1-03

P9-DTT-060

7-01

C is for Clown

A CIRCUS OF "C" WORDS

by Stan and Jan Berenstain

A Bright & Early Book

RANDOM HOUSE / NEW YORK

Copyright © 1972 by Stanley and Janice Berenstain. All rights reserved under International and Pan-American Copyright Conventions. Published in the United States by Random House, Inc., New York, and simultaneously in Canada by Random House of Canada Limited, Toronto. Manufactured in the United States of America.

Library of Congress Cataloging in Publication Data
Berenstain, Stanley, date
C is for clown.
(Bright & early book, #14)
SUMMARY: Describes a circus balancing act using only words beginning with the letter "C."
[1. Circus stories. 2. Alphabet books]
I. Berenstain, Janice, date   joint author.
II. Title
PZ7.B4483Caac   [E]   72-47
ISBN 0-394-82492-X
ISBN 0-394-92492-4 (lib. bdg.)

H   1 2 3 4

Clown.

Clarence Clown.

Cats carrying canes.

Can Clarence Clown
catch cats carrying canes?

Clarence Clown
catches cats
carrying canes.

Collies carrying clubs.

Cats carrying canes
catch collies
carrying clubs.

Clarence Clown
carrying
cats carrying canes
and
collies carrying clubs.

Cows carrying
cakes and candles.

Collies carrying clubs
catch
cows carrying cakes
and candles.

Can Clarence Clown
carry
cats carrying canes
and
collies carrying clubs
and
cows carrying
cakes and candles?

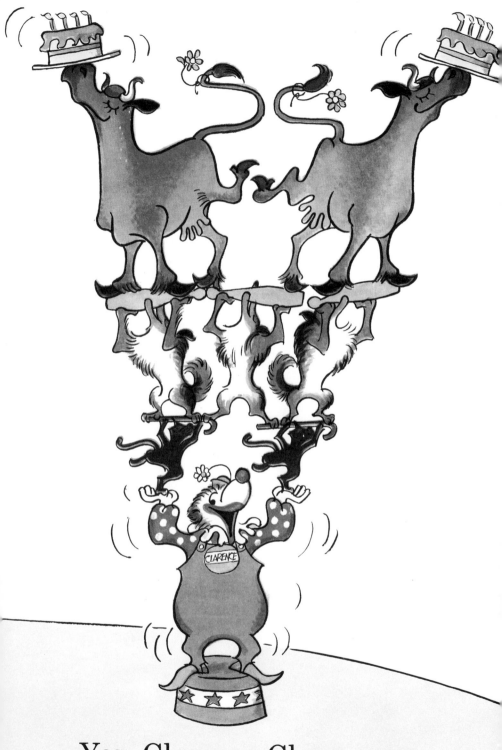

Yes. Clarence Clown can.

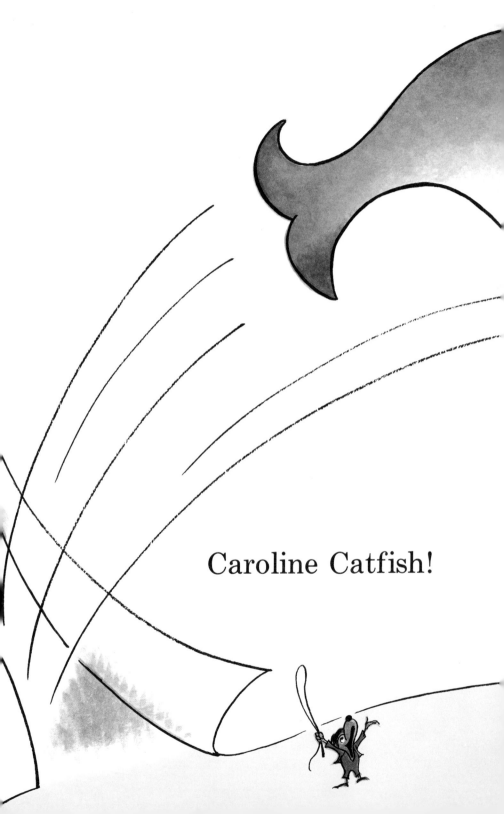

Caroline Catfish!

Cows carrying
cakes and candles
catch
Caroline Catfish.

Can Clarence Clown
carry
cats carrying canes
and
collies carrying clubs
and
cows carrying
cakes and candles
and
Caroline Catfish

and . . .

Clara Canary?

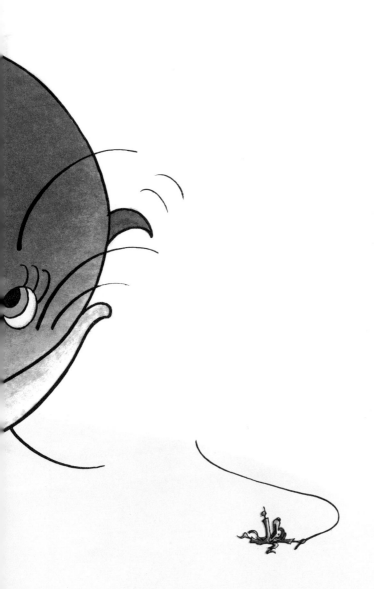

No.

Clarence Clown
can't.